10/13

The SICK DAY

Written by
PATRICIA MacLACHLAN

Illustrated by
JANE DYER

A DOUBLEDAY BOOK FOR YOUNG READERS

The SICK DAY

Special thanks to Juan Romero and
Marlena Candelario Romero
for patiently posing.
—J. D.

A Doubleday Book for Young Readers

Published by
Random House Children's Books
a division of
Random House, Inc.
1540 Broadway
New York, New York 10036

Doubleday and the anchor with dolphin colophon are registered trademarks
of Random House, Inc.

Text copyright © 2001 by Patricia MacLachlan
Illustrations copyright © 2001 by Jane Dyer

Visit us on the Web! www.randomhouse.com/kids
Educators and librarians, for a variety of teaching tools, visit us at www.randomhouse.com/teachers

CATALOGING-IN-PUBLICATION DATA
Cataloging-in-Publication Data is available from the Library of Congress.
ISBN: 0-385-32150-3   ISBN: 0-385-90007-4 (GLB)

The text of this book is set in Parade.

Book design by Alyssa Morris

Manufactured in the United States of America

April 2001

10 9 8 7 6 5 4 3 2 1

After twenty years this book is still
for Bob and Emily—their book, their day.

—P. M.

Also for Bob and Emily
with love.

—J. D.

"I have a stomachache in my head," said Emily. "And a headache in my throat." She dragged her blanket, named Frederick, into her father's writing room.

He felt her head.

"Anything else?"

"My toe hurts where I stubbed it last year," she said. "It hurts on and off. The ons are long."

"You're warm. I think you have a bug," said her father.

"That too?" said Emily, alarmed.

"'A bug' is another way of saying you're sick," her father told her.

Mama was at work, so he put Emily to bed.

"I want Frederick," Emily said.

He pushed Frederick under her chin. She smelled it.

"That's Frederick," said Emily, smiling. "I want Moosie, too."

Father found all her stuffed animals, but not Moosie.

He looked in her closet.

"There's Freda," called Emily. "I want Freda."

"What happened to Freda's hair?" asked her father.

"I cut it," said Emily. "Freda wanted short hair. She told me."

"I wonder where the thermometer is," said Father. He opened Emily's treasure drawer.

"There's my money," said Emily. "Would you put my money under my pillow? It makes me dream of buying high-heeled shoes and plastic jewelry."

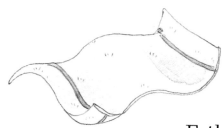

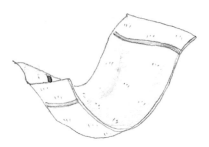

Father went to the hall closet to look for the thermometer. He pulled out all the towels and sheets, but he couldn't find the thermometer. He found Emily's hair elastics with the colored balls.

"Put my hair in ponytails," said Emily.

"Put your hair in ponytails what?" asked Father.

"Put my hair in ponytails, please," said Emily.

Father put three ponytails in Emily's hair. One on top. One on each side.

"You look like a fountain," said Father.

Emily made up a poem about that.

I look like a fountain,
And I look like me.
I look beautiful
In my ponytails three.

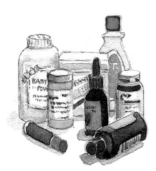

"That's very nice," said Father, smiling. He went into the bathroom and emptied the medicine cabinet. But the thermometer wasn't there.

"My stomach feels bad," said Emily in the doorway. "I think I have to swallow up."

"Wait!" cried Father. "I'll speak to your tummy."

He put his head down next to Emily's stomach.

"Emily's tummy," he crooned.

"Whaaat?" called the tummy in a funny high voice.

"Are you going to swallow up?"

"Nooo," called Emily's tummy.

Emily smiled.

"How come that works?" she asked.

"I don't know," said her father. "Ask your tummy."

"I'm hungry," whined Emily. " And I want Moosie."

"What do you feel like?"

"A cucumber sandwich with mayonnaise."

"That's funny," said Father. "You don't look like a cucumber sandwich with mayonnaise."

Emily laughed so hard she got sick.

Father cleaned up.

"Where's Moosie?" Emily cried.

"Where's the thermometer?" Father grumped.

"Do you think I'm going to die, maybe float up to heaven and fly around with fedders all over me?" asked Emily.

"Feathers," corrected Father. "No, I think you're going to stay in bed and read books."

"I've read them all," said Emily.

"Read them again," said her father in a loud voice. He was looking for the thermometer in the toy box.

"I've read them all thirteen times, and two of them twenty-three times. I know because when I read a book I put a pencil mark up in the corner."

"You do?" Father was surprised. "What a good idea."

 "Would you tell me a story?" asked Emily.
"Tell me a romantic story about a tall man
with lots of hair on his face and not much on
his head."

Emily's father smiled.

"Once upon a time there was a bald prince," he began.
"He fell in love with a sharp-nosed princess named
Princess Pickerel."

"That's the name of a fish," said Emily, laughing.

"No," said Father very seriously. "That's the name of
the princess. They got married and had eleven bald
sons with red beards, and one smooth-faced girl named
Mildred, who had lots of black hair on her head."

"That's nice." Emily rubbed her eyes. "Where's Moosie?"

Father went to the kitchen to look for the thermometer and Moosie. He brought Emily some clear soup.

"I can't eat this," said Emily. "It doesn't have anything in it. I like soup with something floating in it."

Father found a plastic giraffe and dropped it in the soup.

"There. Now there's something floating in your soup."

"Thank you," said Emily meekly.

"You're welcome."

"Paint me a picture of a monster to scare the bug away," said Emily. "A gentle monster."

Father sighed. He brought a large piece of paper into her room and drew a rose-colored monster with wide teeth and a daisy in his hand. Emily smiled.

"It's fun being sick," she said.

Father lay across her bed, with his head way down, looking underneath.

"Are there dragons there?" asked Emily.

"No dragons," said her father upside down. He found two dolls, seven crayons, and a yellow lollipop with hair on it.

"That's Freda's hair," said Emily, who didn't like yellow lollipops anyway.

Father played his recorder for her.

"I like that, the way the notes hop around," said Emily.

"It was written by Bach," he said. "He had lots and lots of children to play for when they were sick."

"Play 'I Have a Mouse,'" said Emily.

"I don't know it."

"I just made it up," said Emily. She sang it for him.

I have a mouse, I have a dog.
The dog would rather be a frog.

Father played it four times.

"It's fun being sick," said Emily. "With you."

The next day, Father found out for himself about being sick. His head felt warm, and he had a sore throat. He lay in bed, and Emily brought him Frederick, Freda, and her money for company. Mama stayed home from work to put the medicine back in the cabinet and the towels and sheets back in the hall closet.

Emily sat on her father's bed and sang "I Have a Mouse" and drew him a fancy picture of Frederick.

And when she lay across the bed and
looked for dragons underneath, she found
Moosie and the thermometer.